JASMINE SPEAKS UP

Jasmine stopped still in the middle of the Pine Hollow driveway. Now she and her pony, Outlaw, were facing May and her pony, Macaroni.

"Don't you see? I don't need you to stand up for me! I can stand up for myself," she told May furiously. "When I want your help, I'll ask for it!"

With those words, Jasmine tugged on Outlaw's lead line and marched right past May and Corey, and right past Lisa, Stevie, and Carole.

"She'll get over it," May mumbled. But inside she wasn't sure. She'd never seen Jasmine look so angry.

Other Skylark Books you will enjoy
Ask your bookseller for the books you have missed

BIG RED by Jim Kjelgaard

ELVIS IS BACK, AND HE'S IN THE SIXTH GRADE! by Stephen Mooser

ENCYCLOPEDIA BROWN AND THE CASE OF THE DEAD EAGLES by Donald J. Sobol

THE GHOST WORE GRAY by Bruce Coville

THE GHOST IN THE THIRD ROW by Bruce Coville

PINHEADS UNITE! (Never Sink Nine #10) by Gibbs Davis

THEY'RE TORTURING TEACHERS IN ROOM 104 by Jerry Piasecki

Pony Tails

May's Riding Lesson

BONNIE BRYANT

Illustrated by Marcy Ramsey

A SKYLARK BOOK
NEW YORK • TORONTO • LONDON • SYDNEY • AUCKLAND

RL3 007–010
MAY'S RIDING LESSON
A Skylark Book / July 1995

*Skylark Books is a registered trademark of Bantam Books,
a division of Bantam Doubleday Dell Publishing Group, Inc.
Registered in U.S. Patent and Trademark Office and elsewhere.
Pony Tails is a trademark of Bonnie Bryant Hiller.*

ISBN 0-553-48256-4

Published simultaneously in the United States and Canada

Bantam Books are published by Bantam Books, a division of Bantam Doubleday Dell Publishing Group, Inc. Its trademark, consisting of the words "Bantam Books" and the portrayal of a rooster, is Registered in U.S. Patent and Trademark Office and in other countries. Marca Registrada. Bantam Books, 1540 Broadway, New York, New York 10036.

PRINTED IN THE UNITED STATES OF AMERICA

/O 0 9 8 7 6 5 4 3 2 1

May's Riding Lesson

1 May's News

May Grover couldn't wait to get to the school-bus stop. She had something really good to tell her best friends, Jasmine James and Corey Takamura. The three girls lived next door to one another, and they all went to the same school, though they were each in a different third-grade class. They were such good friends, they did everything together—especially ride their ponies.

Corey was at the bus stop when May arrived. So was Wil McNally.

"Oh, no," muttered May. Wil was the biggest tease and bully in school. He never missed a chance to tease May and her friends.

May decided to ignore Wil. Instead she talked to Corey.

"Max called my mom last night," May began. "And wait till you hear this!"

"I bet this has to do with your ponies." Wil smirked as he interrupted their conversation.

"Yes, it does have something to do with our ponies," May replied. "Not that it's any of your business. . . ."

That made Wil step back a little. But it didn't make him stop listening.

"Anyway," May went on, turning her back on Wil, "Max called." Max Regnery was the owner of Pine Hollow Stables, where the girls' Pony Club had its meetings. "He wanted to borrow our instant camera. He told Mom we're going to have a special kind of scavenger hunt at the next Pony Club meeting. Doesn't that sound neat?"

"It sure does," Corey said. "But what's a scavenger hunt?"

Wil snorted.

May turned around to glare at him before she answered Corey's question. "It's a game. The leader—that'll be Max—gives us each a list of things we have to find. And the team that gets the most things from the list wins a prize. Best of all, we'll get to do the whole thing on our ponies."

"So what will we have to look for?" asked Corey.

"A scavenger hunt can be for anything," May replied. "Mom said she was on a scavenger hunt once, and she had to get an eagle feather and a 1958 penny. I don't know what Max will put on the list." May glanced at Wil. "But if he asks us to find an obnoxious boy, I know just where to look."

Wil glared at May. She decided not to talk about the scavenger hunt in front of him anymore. That didn't mean she wasn't going to talk about ponies, though.

She and Corey began talking about the riding class they would take that afternoon with Jasmine. The three girls were so pony crazy, they called themselves the Pony Tails. They each had their own pony, and they took classes on Wednesdays at Pine Hollow. Then, on Saturdays, they had Pony Club.

The name of their Pony Club was Horse Wise because that was what the members wanted to become—wise about horses.

Even though they all loved ponies, the three girls were very different from one another. May could be stubborn. She usually said exactly what was on her mind. Not everybody liked that, and it sometimes got her into trouble.

Jasmine was almost a complete opposite of that. She was gentle and a little shy. She had a lot of model horses that she let her friends play with.

Not long ago Corey had moved into the house between May and Jasmine's. Corey was very logical and reasonable. When May and Jasmine couldn't find a way to agree on something, Corey could usually find the way for them. Not only that, she loved ponies and riding as much as the other girls did.

Each of the girls had her own pony. May had a golden-colored pony named Macaroni. Macaroni was as sweet and gentle as May was strong-willed. Jasmine's pony was named Outlaw, because he had a white face that looked like a mask. He was sometimes hard to control. Corey's pony was named Sam, for Samurai. He was a dark bay with a blaze on his face that looked like a Samurai sword.

"I wish Jasmine would get here," May said, glancing over at Jasmine's house. "I want to tell her about the scavenger hunt, too."

"I hope Max puts *brains* on the list," Wil said. "You girls could really use them."

"Is he always like this?" Corey whispered to May. She was still getting to know Wil.

"Always," May sighed.

2 Jasmine's Model Horse

A few minutes later May and Corey heard Jasmine's front door bang shut. Jasmine waved to her friends and skipped down the walk.

May could see that Jasmine was carrying something. It was one of her model horses. Jasmine had eighteen model horses and ponies. May and Corey had some, too. The girls often brought their horses over to one another's house and played with them. Jasmine liked to make saddles, bridles, and all kinds of equipment for her horses. Today she was carrying a model of an Arabian.

"Look what I did!" Jasmine said proudly. She held up the horse to show her friends

the Arabian-style outfit she'd made for it. The outfit even had golden tassels.

"That's neat," said Corey. "Did you do all the sewing yourself?"

Jasmine nodded. "We're studying the Arabian Peninsula in class. I thought everyone would like to see a real Arabian horse. Mom let me use these scraps to make a costume for him."

Jasmine's mother had a big loom that she used to make fabrics from natural fibers. She even made clothes for their family from them. Sometimes Jasmine helped her. She liked to make her own clothes, especially if she could put lace and ribbons on her outfit. Pretty dresses were very important to Jasmine.

Pretty clothes didn't matter at all to May. She didn't care how she looked as long as her clothes were right for riding. Today she was wearing jeans.

May looked at the model horse. As usual Jasmine had done a wonderful job. It looked as if an Arabian king could mount this horse and ride it across the desert.

May's Riding Lesson

The bus arrived. The three girls and Wil climbed into it. May and Jasmine sat together. Corey sat behind them. Wil sat across the aisle from Jasmine next to his best friend, Mark Engstrom.

Jasmine was still talking about her model horse.

"I named him Barq after the Arabian horse at Pine Hollow," she went on. "I even put a streak on his face to look like the real Barq. Did you know that *barq* means 'lightning' in Arabian?"

Corey hadn't known that. She had begun riding at Pine Hollow when she and her mother moved to Willow Creek. And there were still some things she didn't know about Pine Hollow and the horses there.

"I knew that," May said, sounding a little impatient. She was trying to tell Jasmine about the scavenger hunt. But she couldn't get in a word.

"I pretended Barq was a real horse while I was making his costume," Jasmine bubbled on. "He loved it. As soon as I put part of his outfit on, he wanted to prance about and show it off. I finally got him to stand still by telling him he could have some carrots. After that he behaved."

Across the aisle Wil McNally snorted. "Of course he did, he's plastic!" he said loudly. Mark Engstrom stood up to look at the model horse Jasmine was holding. Then he snorted with laughter, too. All over the bus, kids looked around to see what was going on.

Jasmine turned so that her back was to Wil. She jutted out her jaw and kept talking as if Wil weren't even there.

But that didn't keep Wil and Mark from saying things. When the bus stopped to pick up Josh Heffernon, Wil and Mark pointed to the horse in Jasmine's hand.

"Jasmine's a great horsewoman, Josh," Mark said. "She got that wild steed to stand still while she made the costume."

Josh laughed. Jasmine hunched her shoulders.

Wil, Mark, and Josh told Erik Schneider about the horse when he got on the bus. Erik tried to grab the horse from Jasmine.

She pulled it away from him and tucked it in her jacket.

"Be careful," Erik said. "He might kick you!"

Wil, Mark, Josh, and Erik all thought that was very funny. They laughed loudly and slapped their knees.

May couldn't believe that Jasmine didn't say anything to them. She must be waiting to get revenge until we get off the bus, May thought.

The bus came to a stop in front of Willow Creek Elementary School. The door opened. Wil, Mark, Josh, and Erik all stood up to be the first off the bus. May couldn't help herself. As each boy passed her, she stuck out her tongue at him.

That made them laugh, too. But it made May feel better.

At least until she looked over at Jasmine. Her friend had tears in her eyes.

How could those boys tease Jasmine like that? May thought angrily. Wil McNally isn't going to get away with this.

The three girls climbed off the bus and

went into the school building. Just before they each headed for their separate classrooms, Corey took Jasmine's arm.

"You did a really nice job on Barq's outfit," she said. "I wish I could sew the way you do."

"Me too," chimed in May.

Jasmine smiled at them. "Thanks, you guys."

The bell rang, and the girls ran to their classrooms.

Whoops, thought May. *I never did get a chance to tell Jasmine about the scavenger hunt.*

The news would have to wait until later that day.

3 A Very Bad Day

Jasmine clutched her model horse. She kept her eyes on the floor straight ahead of her, and she walked very fast to her classroom. She didn't want to see anybody. She especially didn't want to see the boys from the bus. But Wil and Mark were in her class. She'd be stuck with them all day long.

Ms. Elder was about to close the classroom door. Jasmine made a dash and got there just as the second bell rang. She went straight to her desk and shoved her books inside. She wanted to put Barq there, too, but there wasn't room. Instead she put the model on her desk.

First she heard the sound of a horse's whinny. Then she heard a snort of laughter. She didn't have to look. She knew who had made the noises. Wil had whinnied. Mark Engstrom had snorted. Then a couple of other boys snorted, too.

Jasmine didn't look at them. She stared straight ahead.

"Why, Jasmine, look at what you've got!" Ms. Elder said. "That's beautiful. Did you make the costume yourself?"

Jasmine nodded. She usually liked it when her teacher complimented her. She didn't like it today. She put the horse on the floor by her feet. She hoped everybody would forget about it. Today was not her lucky day, though.

"That's an Arabian horse, isn't it, Jasmine?" Ms. Elder asked.

"Yes," Jasmine mumbled.

"Well, then, it fits right in with something I want to talk about today," the teacher said. "Why don't you bring it up here and show it to the class. What makes Arabian horses different from other breeds?"

Jasmine knew the answer. Arabians were

known for their beauty. They were also known for their endurance. That was what gave them strength to go for long rides in the desert without water or food. They were very valuable horses.

Jasmine knew all this, but she didn't want to say it. She stayed at her desk, while Wil answered the teacher's question.

"Arabians are very different from other breeds," he began. "Even the plastic ones stand still while you put tassels on their costumes!"

Mark thought that was very funny. So did a couple of other boys. Pretty soon all the boys were laughing.

Ms. Elder told them to be quiet. They stopped laughing, but they didn't stop looking at Jasmine. She could feel her face turning red. She didn't say anything about what wonderful horses Arabians were. She didn't say anything at all.

At lunchtime things got worse. Erik came up to her and pretended to be a rearing horse.

"You couldn't sew a costume on me, that's for sure!" he said.

Then Josh called out, "What's for lunch, Jasmine? Oats?"

"Clip-clop, clip-clop," chimed in Wil McNally.

"What dorks," May said. She put her arm around Jasmine's shoulder.

"They don't know anything about horses or ponies," added Corey.

That made Jasmine feel a little better. She smiled at her friends. "Why are the most obnoxious boys in my class?"

Corey and May didn't know the answer.

"It's not fair, is it?" Corey asked.

"No, it's not," Jasmine agreed.

When the bell rang Jasmine took a deep breath.

"Wish me luck for the rest of the day," she said.

Her friends wished her luck.

4 Riding Class

May and Corey knew right away that Jasmine's day hadn't gotten any better. Jasmine didn't say a word while the three of them waited for the bus that afternoon. She wouldn't even talk during the ride. She was completely silent until the Pony Tails got off the bus at Pine Hollow. Then she started talking.

"It was awful!" She blinked to hold back tears.

"The boys didn't stop teasing you all day long?" Corey asked.

"Not for a minute," said Jasmine.

"Well, they're not here," May reminded Jasmine. She gave Jasmine a hug.

"You girls don't have all day to dawdle and talk!" said Max. He hurried past them and went into the stable. The girls rushed in after him. Max didn't like it when students were late for riding class. And today they had only fifteen minutes until their class began.

Corey thought it would be good for Jasmine to be very busy for a while and she was right. Fifteen minutes wasn't much time to change clothes and tack up a pony by putting on the bridle and saddle.

When they had mounted meetings of Horse Wise, the girls brought their own ponies. When they had a half-hour class after school on Wednesdays, they rode the ponies at Pine Hollow. That was because their parents were usually too busy during the week to bring the girls' own ponies to the stable.

Today Max had told Corey to ride Nickel. She was glad about that. Nickel was an easygoing, obedient pony. He always did everything his rider wanted him to do. Sometimes he did it even before the rider told him! He was smart.

May's Riding Lesson

Corey loved Samurai more than anything. She thought he was the most wonderful pony in the world. But lately, he'd been giving her trouble. He wouldn't stand still when she was putting on his saddle and he didn't follow her instructions when she was riding him. Last week he'd even nipped her when she gave him a carrot!

Corey didn't know what was wrong with Sam, but she hoped he'd start acting better very soon. For right now she was relieved to be riding Nickel.

She put the bridle and saddle on Nickel. Red O'Malley, Pine Hollow's stablehand, helped her tighten the girth. That was the strap that held the saddle in place. Then Corey got into the saddle. She was almost ready for class. First she had to touch the good-luck horseshoe. It was a tradition at Pine Hollow. The horseshoe was by the door that led to the schooling ring. No rider who'd touched the horseshoe before riding had ever gotten hurt.

May and Jasmine were waiting for Corey at the horseshoe.

"Ready?" May asked.

"You bet!" said Corey. "How about you, Jasmine? Feeling better?"

"Riding *always* makes me feel better," said Jasmine. She had a smile on her face. Corey was glad to see that.

The first thing Max wanted the riders to do was get their ponies warmed up. They circled the ring four times, walking.

"Now take up a trot," Max said.

Nickel was trotting before Max finished his instruction. And Max wasn't very happy about it.

"You're supposed to be in charge," he told Corey. "Don't let your pony do your thinking for you."

Corey knew Max was right. She had to remind Nickel that she was the boss. Corey pulled gently on the reins. Nickel slowed to a walk. He looked around at the other ponies, which were trotting. His ears flicked eagerly. He shook out his mane. He wanted to trot, too. Corey knew better than to let him do it, though. Instead she made him walk a full circle. Then she loosened on the reins and nudged his belly with her feet. He started to trot. Corey felt good. She'd done it right.

Max raised his hand. Corey knew he was about to tell the riders to circle at a canter. She gripped Nickel's reins. That was a way of telling him he was about to get an instruction. She wanted him to know the instruction was coming from her, not Max.

"Canter!" Max said.

Nickel's head bobbed down and then up. He was starting to canter. But Corey hadn't told him to do it yet. She held the reins tightly. She made him trot halfway around the ring. Then she touched his belly behind the girth on his outside—the side to the wall. It was what Nickel had been waiting for. He began cantering.

"Nice job, Corey," said Max. Corey was pleased that he'd noticed. Max never missed a chance to point out a mistake. His compliments were rarer.

Once the horses were warmed up, Max had the class work on a lot of skills. They worked on riding positions and on starting and stopping. He tested them on hand positions and leg positions. He checked each rider's stirrups to make sure they were the right length. Then Max made everybody show him exactly how they gripped their reins. The class worked hard. Max didn't miss any mistakes!

"Wow, he was tough today," May whispered to Corey while they walked their ponies to cool them down.

"No talking!" Max said before Corey could agree. "Now, everybody, line up in the center of the ring."

Max often had the riders line up when he wanted to talk to them. May hoped he didn't want to complain about how she and Corey were talking.

Luckily he didn't. He wanted to tell them about the scavenger hunt.

"On Saturday we're having a mounted meeting at Horse Wise. We have a very special activity planned. It's going to be a scavenger hunt, but it's going to be a very different kind of scavenger hunt. Be on time and be prepared to work hard!"

May groaned. "Harder than today?"

"Every day I make you work harder than the day before, don't I?" Max said.

It was true. He wanted his students to learn more every time they rode than they had the last time. That was just one of the things the Pony Tails loved about Max.

5 Untacking

"A scavenger hunt! I knew something good had to happen today!" said Jasmine. She unbuckled the girth of Peso's saddle to take it off the pony.

"Isn't it great?" May agreed.

"Max told Mom about it. I was going to tell you this morning, but first you were talking about the model horse. Then Wil McNally, well, you know . . ."

"Yeah, I know." Jasmine sighed. "I wish you hadn't reminded me." She tugged hard at Peso's lead rope to take him back into his stall. Then she realized that she'd tugged too hard. "I'm sorry, Peso." She gave the pony a little hug. "It's not your fault that Wil McNally is so awful."

Peso didn't seem to care about Wil McNally. He did like the hug, however. He liked the water and fresh hay Jasmine gave him even better.

In a few minutes the girls were all done with their chores. It was time to go home. Mrs. Grover drove them in the Grovers' station wagon. All the way home the Pony Tails talked about things they might have to hunt for on the scavenger hunt.

"If it's an old coin, my father has a collection," said May.

"If we need a parrot, I know where to find one," said Corey.

May and Jasmine laughed. Corey's mother was a veterinarian, whom everyone called Doc Tock. She had a parrot that had been left at her office by its owner. Anybody who spent any time with Bluebeard immediately knew why the owner had never picked him up. All day long he made noises like tires screeching or a witch cackling. When Corey had first moved into the neighborhood, May and Jasmine had a hard time figuring out what was going on inside her house!

"Sometimes you need old newspapers on scavenger hunts," said Jasmine. "My parents have lots of those. They save them for recycling."

"I doubt that will be on Max's list," said May. Jasmine thought she was right. She also didn't think a parrot would be on the list.

"If it's not going to be pennies, parrots, and newspapers, I wonder what it *will* be," said Corey.

"If it were going to be easy, Max wouldn't do it," replied May.

Jasmine and Corey thought about the riding class that had just ended and agreed with May. The scavenger hunt was definitely going to be a challenge. It was also going to be fun. The Pony Tails couldn't wait.

6 Samurai Makes Trouble

"Meet you in the ring in ten minutes!" May called as the three girls climbed out of the Grovers' station wagon. "Let's work on some of the skills we practiced in class today."

"Okay," Corey called. She hurried off to her stable.

Shortly after she'd moved to Willow Creek, Corey had decided that Wednesday was her favorite day. On Wednesdays she had riding class, and then when she got home, she rode Samurai with her friends. Ponies needed to have exercise every day. Riding a pony was the best exercise he could get.

Corey waved to her mother as she passed by the window of her mother's office at one side of the house. Her mother was with a patient. She was listening to a cat's heartbeat. She smiled at Corey. Corey didn't have to tell her where she was going. Her mother knew Corey was headed straight for Samurai.

When Corey came into the barn Samurai backed into the corner of his stall. He stomped twice on the floor. He watched her with his big dark eyes.

"It's okay, boy," Corey said. She reached out to pat him. He sniffed toward her hand, but he didn't walk over to her.

This wasn't like Samurai at all. He always greeted Corey with a nod. He came over when she reached out to him. Corey wondered what was on his mind now.

She got his saddle and bridle and tacked him up. He kept trying to move away from her while she put on his tack. That wasn't like him, either. Corey was starting to worry.

She took him to the door of her barn and

lifted herself into the saddle. She nudged his belly with her heels. Samurai didn't move. She did it again, tapping him with the riding crop. Still he didn't move. It took three more tries to get him to a walk.

"Oh, Samurai," Corey sighed. "Something is bothering you and I don't know what it is. You never behaved like this at our old house. Now you're more trouble than Wil McNally."

Samurai snorted.

"Well, maybe not *that* much trouble," she said.

As she and Samurai passed by the house again, her mother stepped out the back door.

"What's the matter with Samurai?" Doc Tock asked.

Corey smiled. It was just like her mother to notice right away that something was wrong with an animal!

"He's in a bad mood," said Corey. "At least that's what I think is wrong."

"A visit with Outlaw and Macaroni might cheer him up," her mother replied.

"I hope so," Corey grumbled. She walked Samurai toward Mr. Grover's schooling ring.

Mr. Grover's job was to train horses. The schooling ring was where Mr. Grover worked with them. Today, while the Pony Tails were in the ring, Mr. Grover was in the stable. He was grooming his number-one student, a Thoroughbred stallion named Vanilla.

The girls began their work in the ring the same way they began their classes. They let the ponies warm up at a walk and then at a trot. Outlaw and Macaroni did just what Jasmine and May told them to do.

"Come on, Samurai," Corey pleaded. "It's time to trot. Don't you want to trot?"

Samurai walked.

Corey knew she couldn't let him walk when she wanted him to trot. That was letting him be in charge. She nudged his belly. He walked. She tapped him with her riding crop. He walked. She clicked her tongue, kicked at his belly, and tapped him with the riding crop all at once. He got the idea. He got it so well that he started cantering instead of trotting.

"Rein him in, Corey," May cried.

"Sit deep in the saddle, Corey," Jasmine called.

"Hold your hands low," May suggested.

"Grip with your legs," added Jasmine.

Corey did all of those things. Samurai stopped.

"I don't know what's wrong with him," Corey sighed. "He wants to tell me what to do instead of the other way around!"

"He's bullying you," said Jasmine. "You can't let him do that. Just like Max said today, you have to remind him that you're in charge."

Corey knew Jasmine was right, but she wasn't sure what to do about it. She didn't want to hit Samurai or hurt him. No good ever came from that. But right now there was no question about who was in charge: It was Samurai.

"I've got an idea," said May.

"It might sound a little strange. . . ."

"Uh-oh." Jasmine groaned and rolled her eyes. Usually May's ideas were crazy.

But Corey listened carefully. After the way Samurai had behaved today, she was ready to try anything. Even one of May's crazy ideas.

7 Samurai Goes to School

"I think Samurai is homesick," May explained. "Maybe he misses his old stable. Why don't we show him what a nice place this is."

"Ma-ay," said Jasmine. "That's the silliest thing I ever heard."

But Corey wasn't so sure. "I don't know what else to do about Samurai. I think it's worth a try."

"First we can show him my stable," May told her. "Then Jasmine's and then yours. We'll let him look around and sniff all he wants. That way he can get used to his new home. We'll let him take as long as he wants."

"Dinner's in an hour," Jasmine reminded her.

"Well, he can take *almost* as long as he wants," May insisted stubbornly. "And best of all, we're going to bring Outlaw and Macaroni along on the tour. That way the three ponies will have a chance to get to be friends."

"Aren't they friends already?" Corey asked.

"Macaroni and Outlaw are, but they've known each other a long time," said May. "Samurai is like the new kid on the block. Sometimes it takes ponies a little while to make friends."

"Like the way it sometimes takes girls a little while?" Jasmine asked.

The three girls looked at one another and laughed. When May and Jasmine first met Corey, it had taken them two weeks to become friends. Now they were best friends. They didn't think anything could tear them apart. They definitely wanted their horses to be friends, too.

The girls led their horses through every inch of the Grovers' stable. Samurai had a chance to meet all the horses who lived there, including Vanilla, Hank, Rascal, and Dobbin. Samurai got to sniff things and look at them. He was very curious. His ears flicked back and forth; he sniffed and snorted. He nipped and nibbled. He even played with a soccer ball that May's sister had left in the barn.

"He's like a kitten," said Corey.

"He's starting all over," May explained. "Everything is new to him."

"This was a good idea, May," Jasmine told her. "I think you were right about Samurai."

May smiled proudly.

Next they went to the little stable behind Jasmine's house. Outlaw was the only pony who lived there. There wasn't much for Samurai to sniff and explore. He looked at it all.

Then it was time to go to Samurai's stable.

"He knows this place already," said Corey.

"But the only part he knows is his stall,"

said May. "He's probably curious about the rest of it."

He was. Samurai looked everywhere. He sniffed in the other stalls. They were empty now, but he still wanted to know what was there. He examined the tack room. He checked out the feed storage. He even started to explore his own stall. Then he snorted happily. He recognized it.

"I think he knows it's home now," said Corey.

"I think he knows more about these stables than we do now," said Jasmine.

"I think it's time to get back to work," said May.

With that, the girls returned to the Grovers' schooling ring.

"Now comes the second part of my plan," said May. "It's called 'peer pressure.' "

Both Corey and Jasmine were surprised. *Peer pressure* meant wanting to do what your friends were doing.

What does that have to do with Samurai? Corey wondered.

"The three of us will ride in a row," May

went on. "We'll put Samurai between Macaroni and Outlaw. If they walk, he'll want to walk. If they trot, he'll want to trot. And so on. It's just got to work."

"Are all her ideas this crazy?" Corey asked Jasmine.

"Most of them are crazier," Jasmine told her. "But sometimes the craziest ones work."

Corey smiled and nodded. So far May had been right. It wouldn't hurt to listen to her again.

The girls lined up side by side.

"First we walk," said May. They walked. It took only three kicks to get Samurai walking.

"Now we'll trot," May announced. Outlaw and Macaroni trotted right away. Samurai held back. Corey tapped him with her riding crop. He started trotting and soon caught up to his new friends.

"I think it's working," said Corey.

"Then we'll keep on doing it every day," said May.

"But it's time to let the ponies rest now," said Jasmine. "Let's groom them."

The other girls agreed, and the three of them tied their ponies to the fence on the schooling ring.

The Pony Tails had quickly discovered that it was as much fun to groom their ponies together as it was to ride them together. Their ponies loved the attention, too.

Each girl had a grooming bucket where she kept tools to clean her pony. First they used their hoofpicks to get any stones out from under the ponies' shoes. Next came the currycomb to remove dirt from the pony's body. Then they used their dandy brushes for legs, mane, and tails.

"Stand still, Outlaw," Jasmine said. "I can't brush the dust out of your coat if you keep moving." Outlaw liked being mischievous.

"It's a good thing you stand still, Macaroni," May remarked. "Your yellow coat acts like a dirt magnet. If you didn't behave, you'd never look clean!"

Samurai stood between the two other ponies. He fidgeted when Corey began to groom him. Then he looked at Outlaw. He

glanced toward Macaroni. Finally he looked at Corey. He stood still.

"Good boy, Sam," Corey said, patting his head. "You're learning. Until you start acting like yourself again, I think we'll spend a lot of time with Outlaw and Macaroni. No more bullying me."

"Speaking of bullies . . . ," May began. She looked over at Jasmine. "What are we going to do about Wil McNally?"

"Nothing." Jasmine shook her head.

"For revenge, I mean," May said.

"Nothing," Jasmine repeated.

"But we can't let him get away with teasing you like that," May insisted. "That's like letting a pony do whatever he wants. Wil will think he's in charge."

"I don't care about revenge, May," Jasmine told her friend. She dropped her dandy brush in Outlaw's grooming bucket. The pony's coat gleamed in the afternoon sun. "I just want Wil to stop."

"The best way is revenge," May said.

"I don't think so," said Jasmine. She looked up. "I'd better go. It's almost dinnertime."

"Jasmine!" Mrs. James called out the front door a second later. "Time for dinner!"

Jasmine waved good-bye to her friends. "I'll see you in the morning."

"How did she do that?" asked Corey as she watched Jasmine lead her pony away. She couldn't believe that Jasmine had known the exact moment her mother was going to call her.

May shrugged. She'd never been able to figure it out, either. "So do you think we should plan some revenge on Wil?" she asked Corey, changing the subject back to Wil McNally.

Corey stopped to think for a minute. May and Jasmine were her best friends, but they had been friends with each other for a lot longer. She didn't want to get in the middle of their disagreement. And she especially didn't want either one of them to wind up mad at her.

"I don't think we should plan revenge if Jasmine doesn't want us to," she told May finally. "It sounded like she wants to ignore Wil."

May shook her head. "We're not letting Samurai bully you," she said stubbornly. "Why should we let Wil bully Jasmine?"

Corey looked at her pony. He was standing so politely now that it was hard to imagine how naughty he'd been before. May had been right about Samurai. Maybe she was right about Jasmine and Wil McNally, too.

"Corey! Come feed the dogs!" her mother called out the back door. The Takamuras had a golden retriever that had a litter of puppies. It was Corey's job to feed them.

"If I were Jasmine, I'd have known she was going to say that," Corey joked.

May smiled. "See you tomorrow," she said.

Corey took Samurai and walked him by his lead rope. This time she only had to tug twice to get him moving.

Corey didn't know what to do about Wil McNally, but she was sure about one thing. Thanks to May, Samurai had gotten some of his good manners back.

8 May Goes to School

Thursday was a special day at school. It was the day of the book fair. May couldn't wait to look for books about horses and ponies.

As soon as May's teacher, Ms. Steinberg, said it was time to go, May bolted from her chair. She ran to the auditorium, where all the books were laid out on tables in a big circle. The first table was filled with picture books for the young kids. Then there was a table of short chapter books and a table of books for older kids. Beyond those were the sections the librarian called "Special Interests." Horse and pony books were there.

May had brought money from her piggy

bank at home. She thought she had enough to buy two books. It'll be so hard to choose only two, she thought. She'd probably need the whole forty minutes to do it.

May looked around for Jasmine. Then she remembered this was Jasmine's day to feed the gerbils in her classroom. She'd be late to the book fair. But Corey was already there, standing at the horse table.

Corey showed May a book she'd chosen. It was a photograph book of all the different horse breeds.

"I have that one," said May. "If you want to borrow it, you can."

Corey put the book back. If she borrowed that one from May, she could spend her money on another book.

"Look at this one!" May said. It was a book about training ponies.

"I've got that one," said Corey. "It's pretty good, too. You can borrow my copy." May was happy about that. Being able to borrow one book was like being able to buy three instead of two.

She picked up another book. It had great pictures. She showed them to Corey.

"Look! Here's a pony that looks almost like Macaroni!" she said.

"He's really pretty," said Corey. "But I don't think he's as well behaved. Look how he's tugging on the rope."

"Maybe you should get Jasmine to train him for you!" a voice said behind them. Then there was an explosion of giggles.

May didn't have to turn around. She didn't have to look. She knew exactly who and what that was. It was Wil McNally and he was making fun of May's best friend again.

"Or does Jasmine only ride plastic horses?" Wil went on.

May felt her face turning red. It was one thing to tease someone in front of them. It was another to make fun of them behind their back.

Before May could stop to think, she dropped the book on the table and swung around. Her hand was in a fist. With one swift motion it landed exactly where she wanted it to land—right in the middle of Wil McNally's face!

"May!" Corey gasped.

BOOK FAIR

Wil fell backward onto the ground and reached for his nose with both hands.

May blinked. What had she done? Revenge on Wil was one thing, but punching wasn't right. She knew better.

Two teachers ran over to Wil. Both of them had tissues. They also seemed to have a lot of sympathy.

"Oh, Wil! What happened?" asked Ms. Elder.

Wil looked at Ms. Elder. Then he looked at May. She swallowed hard. She knew she could be in a lot of trouble. She knew she deserved to be in trouble, too.

"Wil, are you all right?" the teacher asked when Wil didn't answer.

"Yeah, I'm okay," he said finally in a shaky voice. "It's nothing."

"Who hit you?" Ms. Steinberg asked.

Instead of answering, Wil looked around the room.

Why doesn't he just blurt out my name? thought May.

"Nobody hit me," Wil mumbled.

"Nobody?" Ms. Elder sounded surprised.

"But then how did you get the bloody nose?"

"It was a book," said Wil. "I hit myself with it by mistake."

Ms. Steinberg raised her eyebrows. "Some mistake."

Everybody, even the teachers, knew that Wil was lying. Nobody said anything, though.

Ms. Elder took him off to the nurse's office.

May watched him go. Was she actually going to get away with punching Wil McNally—the biggest bully in school—right in the nose?

Why didn't he tell on me? she wondered again. There was only one answer. Wil McNally couldn't admit that a *girl* had punched him!

Maybe punching Wil hadn't been such a bad idea after all, May thought. She'd taught him a lesson *and* she'd stood up for her friend. And the best part was she wasn't even going to get in trouble for it. Wait till Jasmine heard about this!

"Wow!" May turned to Corey. "Wasn't that great?"

"I don't know, May," Corey said uncertainly. "Do you really think hitting him—"

"Wil can't admit that a girl hit him," May quickly assured her friend. "He'll never tell the teachers. It's the perfect revenge!"

"Maybe . . ." Corey turned away from May and started looking at the books again.

May hurried back toward the table where she'd seen the book of photos. But before she reached it, Ms. Steinberg announced it was time to go back to their classroom.

"Oh, no," May wailed. She hadn't even chosen her books yet.

May was almost out of the door to the auditorium when she saw Jasmine coming in from feeding the gerbils.

"Guess what, Jasmine!" May cried. "I got even with Wil McNally for you!"

"What did you do?" Jasmine demanded.

"I gave him what he deserved: a punch in the nose," May said, beaming proudly.

"May!" Jasmine's face turned red, and she looked as if she might start crying.

"Don't worry," May told her friend. "Wil

won't tell. He'll never admit that he was hit by a girl! It's the perfect way to get back at him. Now can you do me a favor?" She told Jasmine about the book with the picture of the pony that looked like Macaroni. Then she held her money out so Jasmine could buy the book for her.

But Jasmine didn't take the money. Instead she stared at May for a minute with tears in her eyes, then walked off.

"She doesn't have to cry," May said to Corey. "I'm not going to get into trouble. I'm really not."

"I don't think that's what she's crying about, May," said Corey softly.

But May didn't hear her. She was looking around the room to find someone else to buy the book for her.

9 Samurai's Homework

"Now keep Samurai close to Macaroni, and he'll go," said May. She and Macaroni were walking ahead of Corey and Samurai in the Grovers' schooling ring. Corey wanted to catch up with May so Samurai would be next to Macaroni. She had to make him walk faster.

Corey tightened up on her reins. It was a way of telling Samurai he was about to get an instruction. His ears flicked back toward Corey. That was a good sign. It meant he remembered she was there. She nudged him with her heels. He stayed at a walk, but his strides got longer and that made him move faster. They caught right up with Macaroni and May. Corey eased up on the reins. Samurai then slowed his pace to match Macaroni's.

"Perfect!" said May.

May was right, and Corey was pleased. Samurai was behaving much better.

"I wasn't sure it would work without Jasmine and Outlaw here," said Corey. "But she had that dentist appointment."

"The lucky girl," said May.

"Lucky?" Corey looked at May. "What's so lucky about going to the dentist?"

"The dentist is Dr. Dutton," said May. "He's really nice. He and his son, Joey, used to live in your house."

"Oh, right," said Corey. "And Joey used to be in Horse Wise, too, right?"

May nodded. "We still miss him."

"I can understand that," said Corey. "I miss some of the kids from my old neighborhood, too."

Just talking about her old house made Corey feel a little sad. She loved her new friends, but she'd moved because her mother and father had gotten a divorce. A lot of things in her life had changed in the last few months.

She smiled at May. "Maybe Joey's made some nice new friends the way I have."

"Probably," May agreed. "I just hope he doesn't teach them all our riding secrets. His new Pony Club, Cross County, is our biggest rival."

"Let's trot!" Corey said suddenly. The girls each signaled their ponies to trot. The ponies obeyed right away.

Corey felt very happy about Samurai. Now her pony was doing just what she wanted when she told him. She felt as if she was in charge again.

Corey leaned forward and patted Samurai on the neck. He lifted his head and trotted on proudly. He liked praise the same way people did. It made him feel good.

A little while later the girls finished exercising their ponies and started grooming them.

"May, you're a genius," said Corey. "Samurai is like a whole different pony. Do you think it's because we let him sniff everything?"

"I'm not sure," said May. "But the reason I thought of it is because Dad usually lets the new horses have a good sniff of our barn when they first arrive." May shrugged. "I guess we'll never know if Samurai was in a bad mood about something else. It might have been a problem he solved all by himself."

"Well, I think that you were the one who solved the problem," Corey told her friend. "So, thank you."

"You're welcome," May replied. "I think I've solved Jasmine's problem with Wil McNally, too."

"I'm not sure about that," Corey said. "I don't think punching people solves anything—"

"Wil didn't tease Jasmine or us again, did he?" May interrupted. She knew she'd gotten Wil off Jasmine's back. It would be a long time before he started picking on her—or any of the Pony Tails—again.

"No . . . ," Corey began. Then Samurai

tugged at his lead. He seemed to want to go somewhere, and Corey was glad to let the subject drop. Somehow she didn't think May would change her mind about Wil McNally.

"You know, I think Sam misses Outlaw. Let's go visit him," Corey said.

"Good idea," said May. "Macaroni would like that, too, wouldn't you, boy?" she asked her horse. He blinked and nodded. May knew that meant yes.

The girls led their ponies over to the James's barn. They opened the door and walked in. Outlaw peered over the top of his door. He nodded a welcome and shuffled his feet.

May and Corey each gave him a carrot.

"Jasmine would do this for you if she weren't at the dentist," May told him.

Outlaw just munched happily.

They patted him and said good-bye, leading their ponies back out the door of the barn.

May glanced at Jasmine's house. Riding was always fun, but riding with Jasmine was always more fun. She missed her.

Then May noticed there was a light on in Jasmine's bedroom.

That's funny, thought May. Jasmine was as good at turning out lights as she was at knowing what time it was. Maybe she was home from the dentist.

May looked again to be sure she had the right room. The light was out now. May decided she must have made a mistake. There was no way Jasmine could be home and not want to ride with her two best friends. No way at all.

* * *

Upstairs in her room Jasmine let the curtain drop back into place. She didn't want May to know she was home from the dentist already. She didn't want to see May at all. She was too angry and upset to talk to her.

Wil McNally had been *her* problem, not May's. Jasmine had wanted to solve it *her* way, not May's. She'd been sure that if she ignored Wil, he'd get tired of teasing her and he'd stop. Now with one punch May had made everything worse. Wil would think Jasmine couldn't solve her own problems.

Jasmine watched May and Corey ride into Corey's barn. She closed her eyes and imagined that May had never punched Wil. She'd be outside riding with her friends now, not sitting here alone in her room.

She loved being friends with May, but why couldn't May learn to mind her own business sometimes?

10 Saturday Morning

On Saturday morning May was the first one ready for the scavenger hunt. She quickly loaded Macaroni onto her family's van, then waited impatiently outside the van for Corey and Jasmine. A few minutes later Corey and Samurai arrived, followed by Jasmine and Outlaw.

"Come on, guys!" May called. "I don't want to be late!"

"We're coming, we're coming," Corey replied.

Jasmine looked down and didn't say anything.

Mr. Grover quickly helped the two girls load their ponies. Then the three riders climbed into the Grovers' station wagon for the ride to Pine Hollow.

"What do you think Max is going to have us find?" May asked. She hoped he asked for a 1958 penny. She'd found one in her father's penny jar the night before. It was in her pocket. Just in case.

"I read about a scavenger hunt where some kids had to find an Alaska license plate," said Corey.

"The Zieglers, who live at the end of the street, went to Alaska last summer," May said. "Maybe they brought a license plate back with them."

Jasmine didn't think so, but she stayed quiet and looked out the window. May and Corey kept talking about what might be on the list for the scavenger hunt.

"I almost don't care what it is we have to find, as long as Samurai behaves," said Corey.

"Don't worry. He will," said May. "He's been perfect for the past two days."

Corey nodded. "He was very good when we put him on the van."

"That's a good sign," said Mr. Grover. "Some horses—even well-behaved ones—hate vans. But Samurai just walked right up the ramp without fussing at all. He was a perfect gentleman."

Corey and May beamed. Corey was pleased about that because it meant Samurai was still behaving well. May was pleased because she was sure it was her scheme that made him behave.

As soon as Mr. Grover pulled into the driveway at Pine Hollow, the Pony Tails were greeted by three older riders.

"We're on the same team!" Stevie Lake called to Jasmine.

"You're my partner," Carole Hanson told Corey.

"Max has paired us up!" Lisa Atwood said to May.

Stevie, Lisa, and Carole were the members of The Saddle Club. They were teenagers and the best riders at Pine Hollow. Max liked to have his experienced riders teach the less experienced ones. It didn't surprise May that the Pony Tails and

The Saddle Club would be together on the hunt.

"Have you been practicing all your skills all week?" Lisa asked May.

May nodded.

"It's not the only thing she's done this week," Jasmine muttered.

Everyone looked at her with surprise. It was practically the first thing Jasmine had said all morning, and it didn't sound especially friendly.

"Oh, really?" Lisa remarked. "What else happened?"

"I punched Wil McNally at the book fair and gave him a bloody nose," May mumbled.

"What?" Lisa looked shocked.

"You punched someone?" Stevie added.

"He deserved it," May explained quickly. Stevie was famous for her get-even schemes, but May knew Stevie would never punch someone. "He wouldn't stop teasing Jasmine about her model horse. She needed my help."

That was all Jasmine could stand. Ever

since the book fair she'd been holding in her hurt and her anger. She couldn't do it anymore. She had to get it out.

Jasmine stopped still right in the middle of the Pine Hollow driveway. She and Outlaw turned to face May and Macaroni.

"I *didn't* need your help," Jasmine told May furiously. "Don't you understand? You hurt my feelings when you punched Wil."

May was bewildered. "You mean I hurt *Wil's* feelings, don't you?"

"No, I mean, you hurt *mine,*" Jasmine insisted.

"I just wanted to make him stop teasing you," said May. "I know that fighting's wrong. I shouldn't have punched him. But I couldn't let him make fun of you. And it did make him stop, didn't it?"

"Well, that isn't the only thing that happened," Jasmine said.

"What else happened?" May asked.

"Mark asked me if I'd paid you to punch Wil," replied Jasmine. "Then Erik and Josh wanted to know why I couldn't stand up for myself." She swallowed hard. "Don't you see? I don't need you to stand up for me! I can stand up for myself."

"Then why weren't you doing it?" May demanded. If Jasmine had punched Wil herself, she thought, it would have saved me a lot of trouble!

"I *was* standing up for myself." Jasmine was yelling now. "In my *own* way—and that way did not include punching! So from now on let me fight my own battles. When I want your help, I'll ask for it!"

With that final word Jasmine tugged on Outlaw's lead line and marched right past May and Corey, and right past Lisa, Stevie, and Carole. She held her head high. She looked straight ahead.

Corey, Lisa, Stevie, and Carole all looked at May. May just shrugged.

"She'll get over it," May mumbled.

But inside she wasn't so sure about that. She'd never seen Jasmine look so angry.

"Horse Wise, come to order!" Max barked at all the riders.

May swallowed around the lump that was gathering in her throat. It was time for the scavenger hunt. She would have to think about this later.

She put her hand in her pocket and felt the 1958 penny there. Would it bring her luck? She needed it, but not just for the scavenger hunt.

11 The Scavenger Hunt

"What's this?" May asked fifteen minutes later when all the horses and ponies had been tacked up. She was looking at a list. Lisa was holding an instant camera and two packs of film. Those were the things Max had given all the teams: a list and a camera with film.

"This is *great*!" said Lisa.

"What's so great about it?" asked May. She knew she sounded grumpy, but she couldn't help it. After her argument with Jasmine, she barely cared about the scavenger hunt anymore.

"Look at the list," said Lisa.

May looked at it. Then she looked again.

There were no eagle feathers, 1958 pennies, or even Alaska license plates. She was about to ask Lisa again what she meant when Max clapped his hands to get everyone's attention.

"Okay now, is it clear what I want?" he asked the riders.

"Not exactly," Corey answered. "This doesn't look like a scavenger hunt to me."

"It's not a scavenger hunt in the usual sense," he said.

"You can say that again," May grumbled.

Max gave her a look, but didn't say anything.

"What you're hunting for is riding skills," he explained. "The lists all show pairs of skills."

May looked at the list one more time. The first thing was "Poor sitting position/Good sitting position."

"You'll be working in teams," Max went on. "The less experienced rider will be the model. The more experienced rider will be the photographer. Your job is to take pictures of the riding skills and bring the pictures back to me. There will be a prize for the best set of photographs, but we'll all be winners because we can all learn from the pictures."

This doesn't sound fun, May thought. It sounds boring and stupid. She knew there were lots of mistakes a rider could make, but it seemed silly to take pictures of them. Couldn't Max think of anything better?

Max directed each pair of riders to a different place around Pine Hollow. They had an hour to photograph all the mistakes.

"We'd better get started," Lisa told May.

"All right," May agreed. She yanked impatiently on Macaroni's reins to get him going. Macaroni yanked back. He wasn't used to yanks. And he didn't like them one bit.

May gave him a mean look. "Come on. We've got a job to do."

Macaroni gave her a mean look back.

"Okay, May, this is where we do our work," said Lisa when they arrived at the paddock on the side of the stable.

"What do I do first?" asked May.

"Get up into the saddle," Lisa suggested.

May grabbed the saddle and some of Macaroni's mane in her left hand, along with the reins. She pulled at her pony and lifted her left foot to put it in the stirrup.

Macaroni didn't like being pulled around like that. He stepped away just as May's toe reached the stirrup. May lost her balance. The saddle slid halfway around the pony's belly. May was left hanging in midair, her bottom just inches above the ground.

Click. Flash. Whir.

"Perfect!" Lisa declared. "We've got a picture of number six: 'poor mounting.'" She put a checkmark on the list. "Now let's get a picture of *good* mounting."

May unhitched herself from the stirrup. She removed the saddle and put it back on again. This time she remembered to tighten the girth. She went to remount Macaroni, but he was nervous and took two steps. Lisa couldn't take a picture because there was no "good mounting" to take a picture of.

"Try to walk him," Lisa suggested once

May was finally on her pony's back. "We'll try to get some of the pictures of 'good walking position' as you go."

May nudged Macaroni's belly. He didn't move. She shook the reins.

Click. Flash. Whir.

"What was that?" asked May.

" 'Poor hand position,' " Lisa called out cheerfully.

"Oh," said May. She kicked Macaroni. He didn't move. She was frustrated and annoyed. She lifted her legs away from his belly to give him a harder kick.

Click. Flash. Whir.

" 'Poor leg position,' " said Lisa. She made another checkmark on the list.

By the time Macaroni did get to a walk, Lisa had made three more checkmarks.

At a trot there were two more. They'd gotten "poor foot position" and "unbalanced seat."

At a canter two more *clicks, flashes, whirs.*

"We've got 'poor jump position' and 'poor lower leg at the canter,' " said Lisa. "We're halfway through and we've only been working on this for ten minutes." She glanced uneasily at May. "We need some shots of good positions now."

May flushed. "Don't worry," she said quickly. "Macaroni and I know what we're doing. This should be easy."

Lisa gave May an encouraging smile. "I'm sure it will be easy."

But it didn't turn out that way at all. By this time Macaroni's mood was as bad as May's. Every time she tried to do anything, the pony gave her trouble. When she dismounted and climbed back into the saddle, he took two steps. When she tried to hold her hands correctly, he yanked at the reins. When she tried to keep her legs straight, he bolted forward. Nothing worked right.

Finally tears of frustration welled up in May's eyes.

"I think you need a rest," Lisa said.

Lisa was a sensible and logical person. May took her advice. She climbed down out of the saddle and faced her pony. Macaroni stared back at May.

"What is wrong with him today?" May asked.

"I was going to ask the same thing about you," said Lisa quietly.

That was the last straw. Without another word May handed Lisa the reins and walked away.

12 Time-out

May didn't know where she was going. She just knew she was going. She saw riders in the paddocks. There were pairs of riders in the outdoor rings. There were pairs of riders in the indoor ring. May went to the tack room. There was nobody there.

The tack room was a small room when it was full of saddles and bridles. There were a lot of horses and ponies at Pine Hollow and they needed a lot of tack. The saddles were stored neatly on racks. The bridles were hung on hooks above them. The reins hung in a tangle. May stared at them. Right now her thoughts were as tangled as the reins.

Nothing seemed to be going right. Everybody was angry with her. Even she was angry with herself. And it was all because of a bully. Wil McNally was the cause of all her troubles!

"May? Is that you?"

May looked up. It was Mrs. Reg. She was Max's mother and the stable manager at Pine Hollow. Mrs. Reg was always finding things for the riders to do around the stable. For a second May thought she might hand her a can of saddle soap. But she didn't. Instead Mrs. Reg sat down next to her.

"Having a bad day?" she asked.

"More like a bad week," May replied.

"Oh, dear," said Mrs. Reg. She put an arm around May. May wasn't sure she deserved a hug, but it felt good.

"There was a rider once," Mrs. Reg said. May knew it was the beginning of a story. Mrs. Reg was famous for telling stories about riders and horses that used to be at Pine Hollow. Her stories almost always had a message. May listened carefully as Mrs. Reg went on. "The rider was working on a course of jumps. The horse was a good jumper, so the rider was surprised when the horse wouldn't go over the first jump. The boy tried again. The horse refused again. And then the horse refused the jump a third time. The horse had gotten spooked somehow. No matter what the rider did or said, the horse just didn't want to go over that first jump."

"What did the boy do?" asked May.

"He took the horse back into the stable, got off him, untacked him, and put him in his stall," Mrs. Reg replied.

"He just gave up?" May asked. She knew it was a very bad idea to let a horse get away with refusing an order of any kind. It gave the horse the idea he could get away with it whenever he wanted.

Mrs. Reg ignored May's question. She didn't like to be interrupted when she was telling a story. Mrs. Reg just went on with her tale.

"A few minutes later the rider put the bridle and saddle back on the horse. He walked him out into the open area of the stable. Then he went right through the course of jumps without a problem."

At that, Mrs. Reg stood up. "I think Max

expects you to be done with the scavenger hunt pictures in about fifteen minutes. Will you be done by then?"

"Huh?" May stared at Mrs. Reg. She couldn't believe how quickly the story had ended.

"I think Lisa is waiting for you," Mrs. Reg added. "See you later, May."

May watched the older woman leave the room. Then she sat alone in the empty tack room for a few more minutes, thinking over Mrs. Reg's story. Mrs. Reg seemed to be telling her to get back to work with a fresh outlook. But was there another message there, too?

May stood up then, brushing some hay from her breeches. No matter what else Mrs. Reg was trying to say, May understood one thing very clearly. She had to get a fresh start with Macaroni.

She grabbed some treats out of the sack of carrots Max always kept handy and hurried back to the paddock. She was ready to return to work.

13 A Change for the Better

When May got back to the paddock, she found Lisa and Macaroni waiting for her. She began with a carrot for Macaroni. Normally she didn't give him treats in the middle of a lesson, but in this case he deserved a treat. He munched happily. He then got a hug.

"I'm sorry, Macaroni, old boy. I was in a crummy mood and I took it out on you." He nuzzled her back. At first she thought he was returning the hug. Then she realized he wanted more carrots. She gave him more.

"And I owe you an apology, too, Lisa. I guess I needed a time-out," said May.

"So did Macaroni," Lisa said. She smiled. "Let's start again."

May petted Macaroni's neck. Then she took the reins and the pommel of the saddle in her left hand, put her left foot in the stirrup, and lifted herself into the saddle. It was a smooth move. Macaroni didn't budge.

Lisa pressed the button on the camera. *Click. Flash. Whir.*

"Looked good to me," she said, pulling the photograph out of the front of the camera. "Now let's try a walk."

May nudged Macaroni gently. He responded immediately.

Click. Flash. Whir.

"Great walking position. Now the hands," said Lisa.

Click. Flash. Whir.

It took only fifteen minutes for May and Lisa to complete their set of matched pictures.

"That's it. We're done," Lisa said.

May smiled with relief. She felt much better now than she had earlier in the day. "Let's go see how everybody else is doing," she said.

May loosened Macaroni's girth and led him back toward the stable. They passed by Corey and Samurai. Samurai was behaving very well. May had messed up a lot of things in the last week, but she hadn't messed up with Samurai. She'd been right about him. He wasn't homesick anymore.

Then she saw Jasmine. Jasmine was finished with her pictures, too. She was grooming Outlaw.

May took a deep breath. She needed to have a fresh start with Jasmine even more than she'd needed one with Macaroni. She told Lisa she'd meet her in Max's office. Then she approached her friend.

"Can we talk?" she asked softly.

"What's there to say?" Jasmine replied. She continued to comb Outlaw without even looking at May.

"I'm sorry," May whispered.

Jasmine turned around. "Really?"

"Really." May nodded.

"I know you were trying to help," said Jasmine. "But—"

"But what I did was the wrong thing," May finished. "It made everything worse, didn't it? I wouldn't hurt you for anything. You're my best friend."

Jasmine hesitated for a moment, then finally smiled. "Thanks," she said. "I accept the apology."

May sighed with relief. Jasmine and she were friends again. "Now there's just one thing left to do," she said.

"What's that?" asked Jasmine.

"Fix things with Wil," May answered. "I have this really crazy idea."

"May!" Jasmine warned her. "No revenge! I mean it. If we ignore him . . ."

Jasmine stopped talking. Now May was laughing. "I'm only kidding," she said. "I really don't have any more ideas."

Jasmine stared at her friend. Could she trust May this time?

"I promise," said May. "I've learned my lesson. I'll never try to help you again unless you want me to." Then May brought Macaroni over to stand next to Outlaw for an extra-special grooming.

14 The Rewards of Hard Work

Max put all the piles of pictures in front of him. There were sixteen riders at Pony Club that day. There were eight piles of pictures. He looked at the first picture.

"Awful!" he said. Then he looked at another. "Dreadful!" Then he looked at the next. "Oh, no!"

"I guess we really blew it," Jasmine said to Corey.

May was getting the uncomfortable feeling that Jasmine was right.

"How could you! No way! Think of the poor horse!" said Max. Then he looked up at the riders in his office and smiled. "This is exactly what I wanted!"

He stood up and took three boxes of pushpins out of his desk drawer. "There's a lot of white space on the wall in the locker area," he said. "I want each team to put up all the pictures there, the good and the bad. Every time you go into the locker area, you'll have a chance to see what's right and what's wrong. Study them and remember to do the *dos* and not the *don'ts!*" He handed the pictures back to the teams who had done them.

Everybody wanted to see everybody else's. Corey had done the worst jump position. Her back was all curved and she practically had her forehead in Samurai's mane. May thought Jasmine's foot position was the worst. Her heels were high and her toes were pointed straight into the horse.

But there, right next to every bad picture, May noticed, was a good one. It showed that the riders knew what was right and what was wrong. And even better, May realized, it reminded her of what she had learned today. That there was a wrong way and a right way to treat ponies as well as friends.

A few minutes later Max came to the locker area for inspection. He stood in front of the wall. He nodded happily.

"Very good, riders," he said.

The members of Horse Wise were pleased. Max didn't say "very good" often.

"Now I want you to know," he added, "this is the last time you'll ever make me happy by riding badly!" The riders laughed. "But because you've done such a good job of being bad, come have some fun being good. Who wants to play shadow tag on horseback?"

They all did.

15 Getting Even

May ran out of her house on Monday morning. She didn't want to miss the bus.

Jasmine skipped out of her house. She was feeling much better now that May had apologized. Sometimes May made mistakes —big ones. But that was over now. They were friends again. They'd even gone on a trail ride yesterday with Corey and had lots of fun.

Corey walked quickly from her house. She waved to her two best friends. Everything seemed wonderful now. May and Jasmine weren't angry with each other. Samurai was still behaving, too. He'd been perfectly polite for the whole trail ride she'd had yesterday with Jasmine and May.

Wil McNally walked out of his house just then.

"Wow, look at Wil's eye," Jasmine said.

"You really pack a punch, May!" Corey whispered.

May turned away. Wil's bloody nose from Thursday had become an ugly black eye. Looking at the eye only reminded her of what a big mistake she'd made.

All morning long in school May squirmed in her seat. Being angry at Wil was one thing, punching him was something else altogether.

At lunchtime May, Jasmine, and Corey ate together.

"How's Wil doing?" May asked Jasmine.

"I think his eye hurts him, but he won't say anything," said Jasmine. She'd been in class with him all morning.

May hung her head. "I feel terrible about it," she said. "It looks so awful."

Corey stared at May. "Did I hear right? *You* feel sorry for Wil McNally?" she asked.

May nodded. "I mean I think he deserved some kind of revenge for being so mean to Jasmine. What makes me feel bad, though, is that *I* punched him. I can't believe I hit someone."

Corey opened her lunchbox and took out her lunch. So did Jasmine and May. Nobody said a word for a while. They were all thinking.

"There has to be a way to fix this situation," said Corey finally.

Jasmine scratched her chin. Corey chewed on a piece of celery. May took a drink of her juice.

"That would take real magic," Jasmine remarked.

"Maybe I should just say 'Hocus-pocus,' " May agreed glumly. "And then it will all be better."

Corey took another bite of her celery. Then she stopped chewing.

"That's it!" she said.

" 'Hocus-pocus'?" May asked.

Corey shook her head. Her eyes were lit up. "Not 'hocus-pocus,' but some other magic words."

May scrunched her eyebrows together. She didn't know what Corey was talking about.

Then Jasmine nodded. "It's perfect," she said.

"What's perfect?" May asked. She was still confused.

"The magic words!" Corey and Jasmine said together. Then they clapped their hands together and said "Jake." Whenever the best friends said the same thing at the same time, they clapped their hands together and said "Jake."

May still didn't get it. " 'Abracadabra'? What would that—Oh, wow!" Now she got it. Corey and Jasmine were telling her to say the magic words "I'm sorry."

She looked from Corey to Jasmine. "You're right. That's exactly what I need to do."

Once May had made up her mind to do something, she always did it right away. She looked around the cafeteria. At Willow Creek Elementary School the students all sat at big, long tables with a teacher at one end. Wil always sat as far from the teacher as he could. Today he was sitting at the end with Josh, Erik, and Mark.

May stood up. Corey and Jasmine stood up, too. They didn't want to miss this.

May walked over to Wil. Corey and Jasmine walked right behind her.

Everybody at Wil's end of the table stopped talking when the Pony Tails arrived. Wil's eyes opened wide—even the black one. He looked surprised to see May there.

"I'm really sorry, Wil," May began. Wil didn't move. Josh, Erik, and Mark stared at her.

"I never should have punched you the way I did. You were being mean to Jasmine, but it still wasn't right for me to do that to you," May went on.

Wil stared at her. But May didn't mind. For the first time since Thursday she felt good about herself. She wasn't quite sure why Josh, Erik, and Mark were staring at her, too, but that didn't matter. She was doing the right thing.

"I hope you won't tease Jasmine—or anyone—anymore, but I promise I'll never punch you again. Will you forgive me?"

Wil gulped. He looked at his friends.

"She did that to you?" Josh asked.

"I thought you said some really *big* kid did it," said Mark.

"A *girl* punched you?" Erik asked.

May felt her face turn red. She'd been so ready to apologize to Wil, she hadn't even thought about his friends. Of course they had no idea that May was the one who'd punched Wil.

Wil grumbled something into his salami sandwich.

"What?" May asked.

He repeated it. It sounded like "Mfprleff-eff."

"Huh?" May replied.

Wil swallowed. "It's okay," he said. Then he slunk low in his seat.

"I think we can go, May," Corey said. She took May's hand and led her friend back to their table.

Behind her, May could hear Josh, Erik, and Mark laughing.

Oh no, she thought. Now I've made everything with Wil worse.

But Corey was laughing, too. "That was

brilliant, May," she said. "You apologized so you don't have to feel bad anymore. And now Wil's friends are teasing him as badly as he teased Jasmine."

May stopped for a moment. Maybe things *had* worked out okay, as Corey seemed to think. She glanced at Jasmine. Was she going to be angry at May all over again?

A big smile spread across Jasmine's face.

"That's a much better kind of revenge, May," Jasmine told her.

"You're not mad?" May asked.

Jasmine shook her head. "Not at all. I have a feeling that Wil McNally is going to leave us alone for a long time!"

16 The Final Lesson

"Watch out for branches!" Jasmine said.

"I will!" said Corey. She ducked under a pine bough that reached across the trail.

Later that afternoon the three girls were riding along a trail in the woods behind their homes. The minute school was over, they'd agreed they had to go on a trail ride. It was a beautiful day, and they had so much to talk about.

The path widened then. The three girls drew their horses in a row and walked together.

"You were great today at lunch," Jasmine said to May.

"Perfect," agreed Corey. "You should

have seen what happened when I took Dracula for a walk this afternoon." Her friends looked at her. Then they remembered that Dracula was a dog. "Wil was in his front yard," she continued. "The minute he saw us, he ran inside!"

May and Jasmine giggled.

"I told you he'd leave the Pony Tails alone!" said Jasmine.

Suddenly May drew Macaroni to a halt. Corey and Jasmine did the same.

"You know what I wish?" May said.

"What?" asked Jasmine.

"I wish there were a way to take pictures of Wil like we did in the scavenger hunt," she explained.

"You mean, like a picture of you punching Wil and another one of you apologizing to him?" Corey asked.

"Yes, that's exactly what I mean," said May. "I don't ever want to forget what I learned."

"I'm not sure you need that," Jasmine pointed out. "You have the Pony Tails to remind you!"

The three of them laughed, and Macaroni

stomped his feet, as if he were agreeing with Jasmine.

"I guess Macaroni won't let me act like a bully, either," May said.

"Sometimes I think Samurai teaches me more than I teach him," Corey agreed. "Doesn't that show how great ponies can be?"

"And how great friends can be, too," added May. She held out her hand, faceup. Corey and Jasmine each gave her five.

"Come on, Pony Tails, let's trot on!" said Jasmine.

May nudged Macaroni with her heels. There was a long trail ahead. It was time to get going.

JASMINE'S TIPS FOR BRAIDING A PONY'S MANE AND TAIL

One day at Pony Club, Max taught us how to braid our ponies' manes and tails. It turned out to be my favorite Pony Club meeting. Even though I have trouble keeping Outlaw still sometimes, I love braiding his mane and tail. He looks so pretty when it's all finished.

Braiding a pony's mane is a lot like braiding your friend's hair. Outlaw's mane looks best when I do eight braids. I divide his mane into eight sections and braid each one. I have to remember which way I start, though, so that all the braids start the same

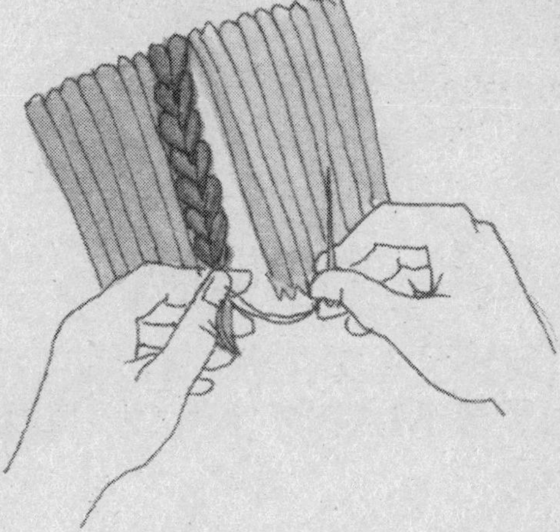

way. It doesn't matter which way, as long as it's the same. Then, instead of having a tassel of hair at the end of the braid, I fold the braid back under itself. I use a needle and thread to sew it in place. (I sew the braid to the braid—not to Outlaw!)

Sometimes, I also decorate Outlaw's braids with ribbons. I tie a pretty colored bow on each braid or weave a ribbon into each braid. On July Fourth, I used red, white, and blue ribbons. I think ribbons look

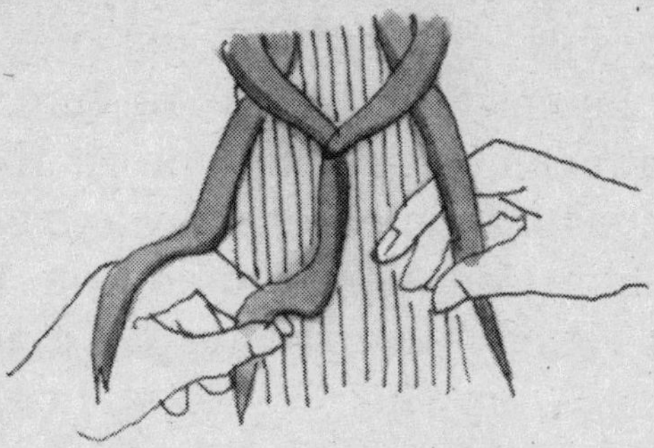

really pretty, but Max says that the braids have to be plain for horse shows.

Braiding a pony's tail is a little different. Once I've brushed (and brushed, and brushed, and brushed!) the tail, I take strands of hairs from each side and begin braiding. At first, I'm just braiding around the bone in the pony's tail. I stop braiding when I'm about halfway down the length of the tail. That leaves the pony plenty of loose hair to brush away flies and to flip around and show off. The last thing I'd ever want to do is to deprive my pony of his very own Pony Tail!

Jasmine's Braids

Outlaw fusses every minute when I'm braiding, so I always try to get him settled before I begin. First I cross-tie him, which means attaching his lead line to the stall. Then I give him some fresh hay and water to distract him from what's going on. Outlaw may not exactly love having his mane and tail braided, but when it's done, he's happy as can be. He holds his head high and swishes his tail proudly. The last time I did it, I was sure he was looking for a camera to smile at. He's so vain!

Don't you just love a pony like that?

About the Author

Bonnie Bryant was born and raised in New York City, and still lives there today. She spends her summers in a house on a lake in Massachusetts.

Ms. Bryant began writing about girls and horses when she started The Saddle Club in 1987. So far there are more than fifty books in that series. Much as she likes telling the stories about Stevie, Carole, and Lisa, she decided that the younger riders at Pine Hollow Stables, notably May Grover, have stories of their own that need telling. That's how *Pony Tails* was born.

Ms. Bryant rides horses when she has time away from her computer, but she doesn't have a horse of her own. She likes to ride different horses, enjoying a variety of riding experiences. She thinks most of her readers are much better riders than she is!